ANYA of MAJADON

to Iyanna and Aria Moffett

Love,
Mrs. Thomas

3.12.22

ANYA of MAJADON

Anya's Remarkable Donkey

"Where your treasure is, there you heart will also be."
~ Matthew 6:21

Deborah Thomas

Anya of Majadon:
Anya's Remarkable Donkey

Sun and Moon Press
Tucson, AZ

Authored and illustrated by Deborah Thomas

Front cover design: Monty Kugler
Back cover & interior design: Benjamin Vrbicek (benjaminvrbicek.com)

Trade Paperback ISBN: 978-1-7338571-2-3
Ebook ISBN: 978-1-7338571-3-0

To our dear grandchildren:
Mariah, Dominic, Cameren, Sierra, Ambrah,
Liam, Layla, Rowan, Aliyah, Callista,
Emmalin and Arabella.
May great stories touch your heart.

CONTENTS

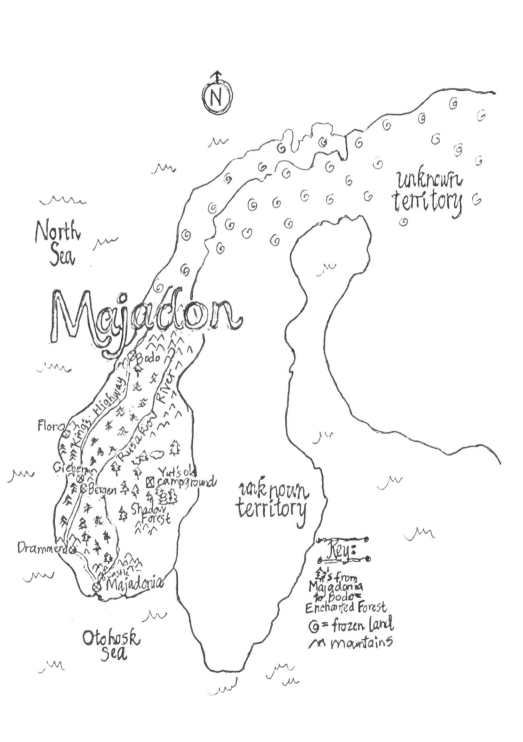

CHAPTER ONE

The Arrival

Long ago in the magical kingdom of Majadon there lived a happy family. First came two boys, next a girl and two wee ones. Gaillard and Freya Tamarkin loved all their children. Anya was the first girl in three generations, and she was brave and adventurous. She loved the outdoors, yet had to be carefully watched, for her fearlessness sometimes introduced trouble.

As often happens with children when they grow up, Anya settled down and became obedient. Her love for the outdoors never changed, and that is where you'd find her every chance she had.

Garth   Anya   Mama   Papa   Katia   Freddy   Garth   Nana

She and her best friend Max were always up to something. They met at the Rusakov River when they spotted Vera, a magical dragon who guarded villagers for the king. Max loved adventure as much as Anya. They were the same age and both had baby sisters. Besides exploring, they liked to dig in the earth and caves, hoping for treasure. They found nothing nearby, and were ready to search elsewhere. Anya dreamt about having a donkey, to go with them.

Some months back, an enemy of the king had caused a disturbance in the kingdom. Yut the Defiant kidnapped babies and used his army and tigers to carry out his evil plans.

Max   Anya

Max and Anya could hardly believe Yut would do such a thing. They had good reason to be alarmed, however when they discovered it was true. Anya's brother witnessed a kidnapping. A tiger grabbed a baby by its collar, raced to a paddy wagon and jumped in. Günter tried to stop them but the soldier drove away quickly while his co-hort held the baby. It turned out to be Max's sister, Danika.

Max and Anya ran to Vera for help because Vera talked and could fly. She reached the castle and quickly reported the kidnapping. The king took action. Yut was warned to stop, but true to his name, he refused. In the end, The Battle in Shadow Forest had to be fought. Yut and his army were defeated and the countryside returned to peace. King Gregory ordered Yut's compound in Shadow Forest burned to the ground.

*   *   *

The peaceful state of Majadon was just how the people liked it.

The Tamarkins were feudal farmers in Bergen and worked a three-acre potato field, giving half their crop to the king. Though they did have a house, they weren't much more than peasants. They were fortunate to have a cow, two horses, ten chickens and sheep. Garth, the oldest, and Günter (the next boy) helped plow, plant and harvest. Mr. Tamarkin was also a carpenter who traveled to sell his wares, so the boys worked harder when he was gone.

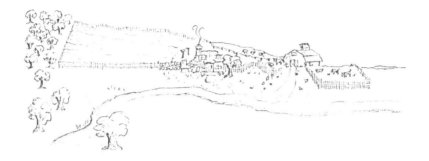

One day something extraordinary happened. Conversation buzzed around the supper table. As usual, Anya was daydreaming about a donkey. She imagined its color and face, and what she'd name it. Her spoon for goulash dangled in midair. The laughter and chatter were interrupted by an unusual sound outdoors. Anya's spoon dropped to the floor with a clank.

She ran to the window.

Father ordered her back to the table. "Anya, it's probably just the local peddler rattling down the lane with his donkey and wares. Come sit down."

Anya cleaned her spoon on her apron, and took another bite. Her brothers watched the window, too. She listened. There was no clatter of wagon wheels.

Instead came some croaky, loud honks and ee-aw's. Could it be? A donkey? Baby Katia started wailing.

Günter burst out, "Maybe it's Mr. Petrov's donkey, Father. He's got a broken gate. Gideon probably got loose and ran down the lane. Can we go and see?"

"Günter, I went by there yesterday. His fence is repaired."

"Then maybe it's a wild donkey," said Garth. It wasn't unusual for donkeys to wander freely down the roads or graze in the meadows of Majadon.

"Papa? We should find out, shouldn't we?" Anya asked. She and her brothers stared at him. Mother's eyebrows arched.

Father dipped his chin, and motioned for them to follow.

Freddy was three, and usually got left behind. "Me go, too?" he said.

Mr. Tamarkin looked at his wife. "Freya, we won't be long." He took Freddy's hand.

Mama nodded.

A white picket fence surrounded the side yard. There, tethered under the shade of a poplar tree, stood a soft gray-brown donkey, its face the color of buttermilk. It stopped nibbling grass and hee-hawed. With its eyes fixed on them, it waggled its head and flicked its tail.

The donkey's ears perked, as they approached.

"My chilblains! Look at those ears!" Father explained that when a donkey's ears were up, it was excited or curious. But when they went down, it was afraid or nervous. He said to be careful, and told them that donkeys could turn aggressive and kick sideways, no matter what was beside them. He untied the donkey from the fence, held the harness and let it smell each one of them.

"Father, this donkey's eyes are bright, and brown. Gideon's are plain and gray. It can't be Mr. Petrov's." Günter had a point.

Father agreed. He measured the donkey's height. "Only ten hands high, not quite grown." On the back and intersecting shoulders of the donkey was a stripe, making the shape of a cross. Anya knew about the stripe because Grandmama's donkey had one and told Anya about its legend. She said all donkeys were given the stripes centuries earlier, when the shadow of a dying man's cross fell upon one little donkey's back.

Freddy stepped closer.

"Freddy!" Father said, pulling him back when the donkey shifted weight. "Stay away from its legs, son."

Garth briskly patted its back. No dust flew up.

"Look at that—a clean coat, son," Papa said. "I like that." He knelt and showed Freddy the donkey's silky white underbelly.

Günter peered underneath. "We can start calling it a jenny," he said. He and Garth bumped elbows and chuckled.

Anya said, "Jenny?"

"Not Jenny! *A* jenny!" Günter said. That's what you call a girl donkey."

The sheep ran to the fence and bleated. The chickens were strutting around before being cooped by nightfall, and clucked. The donkey's ears swiveled, taking in their sounds. The cow heard the commotion, and mooed from the barn. The donkey turned her way. It made them laugh.

Freddy giggled the longest. "Donkey like ar aminals."

Anya pet its back. She said, "Its fur is smooth."

The donkey nuzzled and licked her face. "*Eee-urp—aww.*"

She wanted to feel its mane and ran her hand over it. Something caught on her finger. "Hey, what's this?" A red silk cord was around its neck.

Garth came over. "And something's tied to it!" He went to grab it and Papa took him by the wrist.

"Anya? There seems to be a message attached," Papa said.

She looked closely. What was it? "Papa, you open and read it, will you?"

"To Anya and her family, for bravely fighting evil in Majadon. ~K.G." He turned the note over. 'Her name is Sofie.'

Anya's eyes grew larger than two rubles. "K.G.?"

"Anya, whose initials are 'K.G.' in Majadon?" Papa said. His eyes twinkled. He turned to Garth and Günter and put his finger to his mouth.

Günter said, "Sister, think. Who did you tell when Yut kidnapped Danika?"

Anya gasped. "King Gregory!"

Papa smiled and held her chin. "That's right. He must have thought what you did was important. The donkey's your reward."

Anya threw her arms around her father. "Oh Papa! One for my very own! My dream come true! Now I can hunt for treas—"

"Now hold on there, sis!" said Papa. "You're not going anywhere on your own yet. We'll talk about that when the time comes."

She was about to ask him when that would be when Garth said, "Hey! Anya! Since the donkey's for all of us, how about we take turns?" He was always figuring out how to get the most out of something.

"Are you going to call her Sofie?" said Günter. "Because I know another name, if you like." He was the thoughtful brother. "What about Gunilla? That's a good one."

"No, brother, that's my doll's name." She stood back to study the donkey's face. Sofie bared her teeth, nickered and made them laugh. Anya put her hand out, palm up. Sofie licked it and nudged her other one.

"Papa? I . . . I think she's hungry."

Freddy ran for a carrot. Meanwhile, the boys rode Sofie. Garth went to the road and back. Günter went around the barn with her. Sofie didn't buck either of them.

"Now you, daughter," Papa said. He helped Anya up. Garth walked her up and down the lane, holding the reins. When he helped her down, Sofie turned her head and honked. Anya hugged her neck and spoke to her. "I love you, too, donkey girl."

Sofie raised her head, hee-hawed and squeaked. It made them laugh once more.

Papa directed her brothers to put Sofie in the stall and give her barley. He and Anya and Freddy went back inside.

*   *   *

It was a brighter, lovelier time as they finished supper. Katia played in her pen beside them, shaking her rattle and teething on her blocks. After helping Mama clean up, Anya wanted to rename Sofie. She remembered how they brainstormed names for Marta the cow and thought to try that again.

She got out her slate and charcoal and sat beside Katia. "Now let's see . . . Zuki?" She crossed that out and ran her tongue over her lips. "Zelda? Zenovia? Eva?" She crossed more names out that didn't sound right.

Garth interrupted so she asked Papa if she could sit in the barn, to think better. He said yes, if she kept back from Sofie's legs.

"Hi, pike." (pēk´-yā) Keeping Papa's instructions in mind, she sat a yard away on the milking stool. Just for the fun of it, she introduced Sofie to the cow. Marta mooed. Sofie twitched her tail and answered her with chittering and something that sounded like 'onka.'

"I'm thinking of a new name for you, Sofie." She wrote smaller to fit more names on the slate. "Gretel, Hildegard, and . . . Irina." She paused and worked her mouth. "I think four names is enough to pick from, don't you?"

She asked her family and friends to vote. Mama picked Irina. Papa wanted Zenovia so they could nickname her Novi. Grandmama chose Hildegard and so did Günter. Garth said voting was silly. That she should just pick any old name and he didn't care what.

That didn't stop Anya. She would ask other people and never mind Garth.

She could hardly wait to show Max the king's gift. She and Günter walked Sofie to Geiben where he lived. (She couldn't take Sofie all by herself yet.)

After Max and his family voted, Günter walked them to the river and they found Vera. Vera's brother Vicente was there, so he voted, too. On the way back, she asked Mr. & Mrs. Petrov which name they liked.

At home, she tallied the votes. Zenovia got two, Hildegard five, Gretel three and Irina five. It was down to Gretel, Hildegard, and Irina. She repeated the names slowly. Maybe Papa or Grandmama knew what they meant. It so happened that Gretel meant pearl, and Irina meant peaceful. 'Hilde' stood for battle, and 'gard' for protection. Like a battle maiden. Anya liked the names Hilde and Irina the most.

She made up a test to see if Sofie would come to her, at the sound of one of the names. In the barn, Anya brushed her and explained things. "Now listen, donkey. Today I'm going to name you. Please cooperate." Anya used a low voice with her. "I want you to pick one of these names. All right?"

Anya wrote the names' initials in the dirt five feet from Sofie. Sofie's ears twitched.

She shut the barn door, and opened her stall. "Ready? When I say a name you like, come stand in front of me. Understand?"

The donkey cocked her head.

"Here we go." Anya stood behind the 'I' and said, "Irina."

Sofie did nothing.

"Okay, that's no. Here's the next." She stepped behind the 'H' and said Hildegard. The donkey flipped her tail, made a graveled sound and burrowed into her stomach.

Anya giggled. "So, you like 'Hildegard'?"

The donkey nodded.

"Well, there's one more." She led Hilde back to her stall and told her to stand still. When Anya stood behind the letter 'G,' she said, "Gretel."

Sofie gave a snort, brayed and shook her head from side to side.

Anya laughed. "Okay, *not* Gretel!"

She repeated 'Hildegard,' then 'Hilde.' The donkey flicked her tail, made a happy 'ee-aw' sound, and walked over. Anya hugged her. "Then, you're Hildegard! Your name means protection and battle-maiden. You and I'll protect Majadon together!"

Hilde nudged her, found her hand and nibbled her palm, and said, "*Yäh!*"

Anya startled. "What? Hildegard, did you just speak?"

Hilde nodded and said, "*On-ya.*"

"Did you say Onka?"

Hilde shook no. "*On-ya.*"

Anya sat down hard. "You said MY NAME?" What other words did she know?

Hilde moved her head up and down, twice.

Anya stood up. She pointed to Hilde's chest and said, "Hildegard."

The donkey said '*Hildegard.*'

She pointed to her own chest. "Anya."

Hilde said '*Anya.*'

"Oh, my goodness!" Anya tickled her muzzle and gave her a treat. She put her in the stall and ran inside to tell her family Hilde's new name.

CHAPTER TWO

The Lesson and The Forest

Anya didn't tell them Hilde could talk. Not yet. She had to be sure it wasn't her imagination.

She awoke before the rooster did, and dressed quickly. Mama and the little ones were still asleep. Papa, Garth and Günter were eating sausages and hot cross buns at the breakfast table. Anya kissed Papa goodbye. She and Günter went to feed and bridle Hilde for her first lesson at Grandmama's.

"Oh fiddlesticks!" said Günter. "Look what she did!"

Her feeding bucket was chewed to pieces on one side.

"That's what you get for leaving it in her stall, brother." She still scolded Hilde.

Anya couldn't wait to go to Max's. Her plan was simple. After the lesson, she and Günter would go to Gieben. There, Günter would sell his eggs door to door while Anya and Max hunted for treasure with Hilde.

Grandmama made Anya and Max sit down and have latkes, applesauce and milk. Günter already ate and offered to rake the corral for his grandmother.

When Günter went out the door, Hilde brayed loudly.

"Well, if that isn't just like a donkey," Grandmama said. "Never satisfied! Always wanting to be where the fun is! Finn acts the same way!"

"Where *is* Finn, Grandmama?"

"At the neighbor's, down wind," she said. "Donkeys can smell each other a mile away. If Hilde got a whiff of him, there'd likely be no lesson today."

They laughed. Her grandmother had a funny way of talking and Anya loved it.

Anya washed her hands and came alongside her grandmother. She wanted to ask her something.

"Grandmama, I've been meaning to ask . . . can I call you a name that isn't so long?"

Her grandmother chuckled. "Like what, dear? I don't like being called Grammie or Granny. So don't suggest that."

"What did Mama call you, when she was little?"

"Mum. And she called my mother 'Nonni.'"

"Well . . . how about Grandmum or Nonni? Can I call you either one of those?"

Her grandmother laughed full-heartedly. "Yes, you can. I like both those names!" Grandmum put her hand on Anya's shoulder. "Honey, would you bring these carrot pieces along? For Hilde's training."

They went to the corral. "The first thing you teach any respectable animal is to come when they're called. For their safety as well as for yours." Grandmum began the lesson. She put Hilde in the center of the corral and said to her, "Stand still." Hilde did, and received the first carrot piece.

Grandmum walked five feet away and looked directly at Hilde. She picked up a bucket of oats, and said, "Come."

Hilde stood there and stared.

Her grandmother shook the bucket and repeated the command. Hilde's ears perked—she watched but didn't budge. Grandmum said it again. "Come."

Hilde came. With Grandmum's patience and persistence, Hilde obeyed quite well.

"Anya, your turn," she said.

Anya coaxed Hilde with the carrots. She did almost as well for Anya as she had for her grandmother.

"Well done, Anya," Grandmum said. "That's enough for today."

She petted Hildegard's head. "Good girl, Hilde!"

Hilde chattered and pushed into her grandmother's chest.

"Next time, we'll teach you 'Step.'" (The donkey command to start walking.)

"Very well. Thank you, Nonni," Anya turned to Günter and explained the 'Nonni' name.

"Yes, thank you, Nonni," Günter parroted. He tipped his hat, took Hilde's rope and he, Anya and Max headed to Gieben. Anya put her hand in her brother's. She was thankful Günter went along with Grandmum's new names.

The day was cool: perfect weather for carrying eggs in padded baskets. When they reached Max's house, Günter told Anya to wait there until he got back from egg selling. "Now listen, Anya. I don't mind if you walk Hilde to the road sign and back, but no farther. Understand?" He laid his hand on her shoulder.

Anya didn't want to disobey him, after all, he'd been so kind. She was a strong-willed girl, however. She gave him the slightest nod she could without being compliant, and brushed her guilt aside. When Günter was out of sight, she said, "Max! Come on! We have to hurry!"

They set off toward the North Sea beach, beyond a high knoll. They climbed a worn path. Both sides were overgrown with tall grass and peppered with rocks, like the borders of the river. Soon Hilde strained against the rope. Her ears flicked and she vigorously shook her head. She began to trot, and Anya and Max could barely keep up.

At the crest of the knoll, the path split. They stopped. Straight ahead was the beach. They went right, on a path rising sharply toward a mountain. The landscape changed abruptly from tall grass to prickly bushes and soon, fat trees. Hilde climbed more slowly, and it was a relief to the children. Now closer, Anya studied the trees. There was a piney odor in the air, yet the trees weren't pine. The trunks were so wide, a tunnel could be carved in them. She touched the reddish bark and tried to break off a piece to ask Papa about, but it didn't budge. She yanked it harder. Something screeched, and the branches waved menacingly.

She jumped back. Max ran behind a bush. "Max! Get back here! These trees can't hit us or . . . or . . . chase us!" She wanted to sound brave, but goosebumps rose on her legs and arms.

Max stepped out of his hiding place. She took his hand and held it tight. They returned to the path. The tree branches quieted. Was the tree warning them of something? Or trying to scare them away?

They barely walked ten steps when Hilde balked and sat down. Her eyes went to the tree.

At the base of the trunk, a door appeared, backlit by glowing embers. Anya ran to it, and reached for the handle. The branches waved again and a force she could barely describe pushed against her hand. In a snip-snap, the door disappeared.

"Max? Did you see that? Where'd it go?'

"It's probably still there, only we can't see it. It might be a dwarf's house. They can make things invisible. But I don't know if they did this, or if it was nature."

"Nature?"

"Yes. You know Majadon's known for its magic. Remember the mist in the river that came out of nowhere? And what about Vera and her brothers? Flying dragons don't live in every kingdom, you know."

"Mmmm, clever of you to remember that, Max. I better pay more attention." She looked skyward, then sideways, and rubbed her arms. The goosebumps left. "Still, I've never seen a tree like this before, have you?"

"No, but I believe it." He snapped his fingers. "Wait! My uncle said that when he was young, this was called Mystic Forest."

"Mystic Forest . . ." she said quietly. "It's living up to its name."

She locked eyes with Max. "Max, let me ask something. If you believe in nature's magic, would you also believe that—"

Hilde pulled; the reins went taut. She said, "*Time for go!*"

Max's eyes popped. "Hilde can T A L K?!"

"That's what I started to tell you! Until now, she's only said three words. She must be learning new ones, a little at a time."

Hilde nodded, "*I good learner.*"

They laughed. Max pet Hilde. "You are that, Hilde!" He shook his head. "A talking donkey in Majadon! We better keep this a secret."

"How? "Anya said. "She talks when you least expect it!"

"*Anya funny!*" Hilde said.

"See what I mean?" They laughed again.

Back on the path, they hadn't gone four steps when the ground glistened. And gave off a crackling sound. What? More magic? Was this another alert from the forest? There was no breeze, yet the branches waved and the trees whispered.

Anya made Hilde stop. "Wait, Max. Listen."

Something out of the ordinary hung in the air. Birds called loudly and chirped. Some branches rustled, and a short, stout figure stepped out of the forest upwind of them. The man didn't look behind him. An ax was in his right hand and he carried chopped wood in the crick of his other arm.

Hilde lunged against the rope, and brayed.

The little man spun around, and dropped the firewood. "Well, look here! Sofie! How *are* you, girl?" His voice was higher than Papa's. He came nearer. "Hello! Welcome to Mystic Forest."

So, this *was* its name! Hildegard didn't speak, but her ears stood up. The little man tickled them. Hilde pulled towards him.

He said, "There now, there now."

Hilde calmed down.

This time, it was Max who wasn't afraid, while Anya kept her distance. To start with, the man wasn't much taller than they. He had a shortened body and a bushy beard. He wore a floppy gray hat and matching soft moccasins. They looked to be made of elk skin like their shoes. She didn't see any weapons on his belt, but he did have pockets. No telling what was in them. And he was still holding the ax.

Anya had never seen a short person like this before. She stepped behind Max.

"It's alright, Anya. He's a dwarf. A friendly one."

"How do you do? My name's Baugi." He looked directly at Anya. "From the way you're staring, dear, I'll guess you've never seen a dwarf before."

"No, sir, I haven't. Sorry for staring." She lowered her eyes.

"That's all right, I'm used to it. But don't call me sir," he said. "Just Baugi. We sold the king this donkey. We breed and raise them, so this was her home until last month." He smiled. "What are your names?"

Max introduced them and asked, "Did you deliver Hildegard to the Tamarkins for King Gregory?"

"Yes, we brought her before sunset and tied her to a white picket fence."

"With a note on a red silk cord?" Anya said.

"The king's emissary gave us that, yes, and we put it on Sofie."

"I see. But . . . Baugi, I don't actually call her Sofie. I named her Hildegard."

"Hildegard? Well, I like that—I think that name means protector of good." Baugi gave Hilde two pats on her side.

Anya nodded. "And battle maiden." She was relieved he liked Hilde's name.

Max said, "I didn't know dwarfs raised donkeys. My father said they're just metal workers and miners. He should know. He makes minecarts."

"He does, does he?" Baugi rubbed his chin. "Then, might his name be . . . Arman?"

Anya saw Max's eyes brighten and his chest swell up. She chuckled.

"A fine carpenter and metal fashioner your father be," said the dwarf. "And as for our work, young man, your father's almost right. Our men and women are metal workers and also raise donkeys and craft wood. But only the men do the mining."

Anya's brow furrowed. "Then why haven't I seen dwarfs in Bergen?"

"You mean you haven't heard that dwarfs live in the mountains and trees along the King's Highway, Anya?" said Max.

"No," she said. "I had no idea they were in Majadon."

Baugi said, "We don't conduct business in Bergen, Anya, on account of no minerals there. But if you keep exploring, you'll see a lot more dwarfs. I'm sure."

"Oh." Finally, things were making sense. Baugi's friendliness helped her remember her manners. "Thank you for Hildegard, Mr. Baugi. I love her."

Baugi invited them to his village. But it was late.

Anya said, "We'll come another time."

"All right; you can meet my family then. My three children would like that."

Anya looked up. "What are their names?"

He told them.

They thanked Baugi and turned back to Gieben.

Anya liked good conversation. "Max, doesn't your father do woodworking with my father?"

"He used to, but minecart orders keep him too busy now."

"Oh. What kind of minerals are in Gieben anyway?" she asked.

"So far, just zinc."

When they got to Max's, he fed Hilde an apple and Anya watered her.

Günter arrived. "Here I am! Hope you weren't bored while I was gone. What'd you do?"

"Well, we wanted to hunt for treasure," Anya said. "But we couldn't."

"Yeah," said Max. "We never even made it to the beach."

Anya hoped Max's words made Günter think they'd stayed in Gieben. Max wasn't lying since it was true they never made it to the beach.

"Mama's going to be happy I sold all the eggs—except these." He handed Max the extras. "For your family, Max. Thanks for keeping Anya out of trouble."

Günter took Hilde's reins, helped Anya mount, and away they went. She turned around to share a giggle with Max, muffling her mouth with her hand.

CHAPTER THREE

Hilde Finds a Job

Hildegard worked her way into the Tamarkin family's heart in no time at all. She made all kinds of donkey noises, was good natured, and didn't bite, even when Freddy pulled her mane or poked her in the eye. She would simply object with a very loud noise. Then he stopped.

Anya could hardly wait to meet Baugi's family. He had two girls.

And she wanted to tell him how much Hilde helped their family. She was good at guarding the sheep and cow. No more foxes, wild dogs or bears to bother them anymore. Hilde raised a ruckus threatening intruders until they ran off. She was fearless. The horses were meadowed on the other side of the barn. They squealed if intruders came. They couldn't protect the sheep and cow, and were happy that Hilde now did.

The sheep and cow were so fond of Hilde that if she was gone too long, they waited in the barn for her return. Sometimes they bleated and mooed. Their singing lulled Katia and Freddy to sleep at naptime.

Mama took over Hilde's training, to make things easier on Grandmum. She taught her 'Whoa,' how to trot slowly, and back up. Günter and Anya practiced the newest commands with Hilde: 'Gee' for turning right and 'Haw' for left. Mama's experience with horses helped Hilde learn quickly. During the second lesson, Hilde talked. She startled Mama so badly, she stumbled and nearly fell over. She ran to get Papa; he was flabbergasted, too.

Hilde became remarkable and not only because she could talk. Besides guarding their stock, she sometimes worked as a pack animal for them. They wondered how they'd ever gotten along without her.

Anya now took Hilde on short runs to Grandmum's and up the road half a mile in either direction. The commands Hilde obeyed were: Stand still, Step, Come, Whoa, Trot, Back up, Gee and Haw. Papa finally agreed to let Anya travel farther with Hilde, if Max went, too.

They made plans to return to Mystic Forest and dig. When Max arrived the following morning, they headed to the barn. Hilde was gone. There was no sign of her anywhere. Anya slid to the ground in a heap. She laid her fingers across her eyes, to keep from crying.

Max sat beside her.

"What'll we do, Max? Mama left early to bring a neighbor some food. Papa's in Drammend."

"Why don't we ask Vera for help?"

They ran straightaway to the river and hollered. Vera didn't appear, and they sat down to think. The river that morning was as still as a mill pond on Sundays.

"Maybe she's patrolling the highway or forest," Max said. He reminded her that dragons have excellent hearing. "We could yell for her along the road."

"I got a better idea." Anya ran home for her flute, climbed a hill and played as loudly as she could.

Vera flew in before the song was over. "Anya! Max! Hilde was looking for me! She wanted to get acquainted and ask me about my job. And about Yut and his army. She asked me if I fought in the Battle of Shadow Forest."

"What? How would she know about The Battle?" Anya said.

"Wasn't her mother there with the village fighters?"

"Oh. Well, what'd you tell her?"

"That I *did*, of course! And that it was one of King Gregory's greatest triumphs."

"What'd Hildegard say then, Vera?"

Vera cleared her throat. "Well, Max . . . she looked sad. Her head went down and she mumbled something like, '*I wish . . . but I be too little.*'"

34

Anya felt sorry for Hilde.

"Anya, I think Hilde wants to protect the villagers. I told her Shadow Forest was a terrible battle, but now that the kingdom's peaceful, she's older and could start serving the king. She could look for signs of trouble in Majadon, and report it."

"You mean . . . be a spy?"

"Yes, but the good kind, the kind that watches out for evil, to protect people."

"Oh Vera, Majadon's way too big and wide for a young donkey!"

"Then . . ." said Vera, "perhaps just around Bergen."

Anya nodded.

"By the way, Hilde was excited about this idea."

Anya looked around. "Where is she now?"

Vera pointed toward Gieben. "She went that way."

Anya and Max exchanged glances and said, "Baugi!" They ran to the North Sea and started up the path. There were donkey tracks. Soon they heard voices and laughter. They hurried along and saw Baugi leading Hilde. Two little girls were on her back.

"Hildegard! You naughty donkey!" Anya scolded her.

Hilde squawked and sidestepped to get away.

Baugi interrupted. "Anya, let me tell you something about this animal. Hilde's no ordinary donkey so she can't behave like one. She just wanted to see her mum today."

Anya's brow furrowed. "How do you know she's not ordinary?"

"Because today, after she used donkey talk with her mother, she used people talk with me. I had no idea she could do that. Did you know she wants to be a spy for the king and protect Majadon?"

Anya drew in her breath. "Vera just told us, Baugi!"

A sinking feeling came over Anya. She realized she'd never quite "own" Hildegard. How often would Hilde be gone, working for the king? Would they ever have time to hunt for treasure? Her heart felt low.

Baugi read her mind. "It's all right, Anya. Hilde's too young to work much. The king won't let her go far. He has Vera, Vicente and Vladimir guarding things constantly."

The donkey put her head under Anya's arm. *"Hilde love Anya. Hilde want protect her."*

Anya couldn't keep from crying into Hilde's mane.

"Baugi's right, Anya. Hildegard will be loyal, and she'll have time for you." Max patted her on the shoulder.

Baugi gave Anya a moment. She wiped her face with her handkerchief. When she looked up, it was into the eyes of the little girls, who had tears of their own. She apologized for crying. Baugi said she didn't need to. They turned Hilde around and went up the path.

They came to the village clearing, a town square surrounded by wide trees; each tree had a door. Baugi walked to the third one, and led them around back.

There in a corral stood Amáre. Hilde was her mother's spitting image. Their coats and faces were nearly identical. Both had brown crosses on their backs. But Amáre had a buttermilk tail with a brown tip, and her ears were larger than Hildegard's. She nuzzled Hilde in between the corral barriers.

Anya felt happy and looked at Baugi.

He chuckled. "They never tire of that." He opened the corral and Hilde went in.

"Shall we go inside?" Anya and Max followed Baugi and met his wife. Embla put biscuits and cider on the kitchen table and they all ate. Njord stood up and invited Max to cut wood with him. They went outside.

Baugi left for his afternoon shift at the mine. Embla told her girls to get their playthings and follow her to the stream to do laundry. Anya, Eisa and Eir played with their rag dolls and a makeshift wagon of tree branches and scraps of wood. They pretended it was a baby carriage. Anya wished she'd brought her doll, Gunilla.

At home that night, Anya told her family all she discovered that day about Hilde. When she finished, they shared a long silence. Somehow, they knew they'd never look at Hildegard the same way again.

CHAPTER FOUR

Hunting for Treasure

Anya and Max were meeting halfway between their villages to finally hunt for treasure without interruptions. Mama let Anya pack a picnic lunch and Max's mother sent krumkake cookies filled with baked apples. Anya packed cloth napkins, a blanket for a tablecloth, and clay plates so they didn't have to eat out of their laps. They carried milk in a goatskin bag.

She dreamt of finding gold, not for herself but to make her parents rich. And build a bigger house so Grandmum could move in, and hire a farmhand so Papa wouldn't have to work so hard. If she never found gold, Anya's second wish was for peridot, a newly discovered gem in Majadon. She was tired of some folks looking down their noses at them for not having money. If they struck a vein of peridot, she could still make their life better.

To search for minerals, they had to be careful. Caving was serious business. Papa set tight limits. He took them to Gieben mine, on a dry run to teach her and Max safety. They were not to go into a cave any farther than where they had light. Papa didn't trust them with a lantern and said no children had any business poking around in the dark, or stepping into holes, or worse.

This didn't scare Anya. She was a brave girl, most days.

The night before, she checked the wagon Papa built. It held a box for their upcoming treasures. In it, Anya put her leather hat and a canvas backpack of small digging tools.

Max said to wear hard toed shoes so she borrowed a pair of Günter's even if they were too big. Anya didn't much care what people thought of her clothes or shoes, but she did pay attention to her hair. If it was disheveled, it put her in bad mood. She brushed it often and braided it, or held it back with ties.

Max was in charge of bringing the larger tools. When he arrived, she was glad to see a pick axe, shovel, a hammer, claw and a chisel. And two pairs of gloves.

They walked to the barn, to harness Hilde. Surprisingly, she wasn't there or in the pasture. The gate was closed, and since Hilde couldn't jump the fence, she must have found another exit. Did she escape when the chickens went out? Anya didn't feel like looking for her. Maybe this time, she and Max would hunt for treasure by themselves.

Anya found Mama at the clothesline and helped her hang the last of the clothes, before leaving. While pinning up Katia's diapers, she heard the 'Onka' sound. They looked to the road. Mrs. Petrov was walking a donkey toward them, at a distance. Was it Gideon or was it Hilde?

In moments, Anya recognized her pet. Hilde went to Anya and touched her nose to her waist. She nibbled her tunic. She pushed her head under one of Anya's arms and said, "*An-ya!*"

Mrs. Petrov was aghast. "Did I just hear that donkey say your name, Anya?"

Anya was going to answer when Hilde said, *"Hilde see Nonni."* Plain and clear.

The look on Mrs. Petrov's face was priceless. The neighbor patted her chest to regain her breath. "Your donkey *can* talk!"

There was no hiding it, so Mama downplayed it. "Well, I guess we needn't be surprised! If Majadon has flying dragons that talk, why not a talking donkey?"

She turned to Hilde. "Hilde, you are a most remarkable creature!"

Hilde pumped her head in agreement. "Takk-skal-du-ha."

Both Mama's and Mrs. Petrov's eyes bulged.

Anya's too. "Hilde, how do you know that word for thank you?"

"Hilde hear flower girl say."

There wasn't time to waste. Anya would ask Hilde on their treasure hunt why she went to Nonni's. She took her reins to lead her off when she heard Mama ask Mrs. Petrov to keep quiet about Hilde, for the safety of both villages. Anya paused to hear what else Mama said.

"If word gets out, Tuva (Mrs. Petrov's first name), and someone steals Hildegard, she can no longer guard us." Mama touched the lady's arm lightly. "May I offer you some tea and scones? To thank you for returning Hilde? Please come in for a few minutes."

Anya imagined her mother would ask Tuva how long Hilde had been with them. She hoped Mama wouldn't tell her Hilde was a spy.

Anya fed Hilde, and they went south for their first dig. They saw some ruins, overgrown with grass. They dug up pottery shards and a wooden spoon. While digging, they heard a rumble and the ground moved, for a brief spell. There were no signs of a coming storm. They went north and nearing the Petrov farm, heard donkeys braying. They followed the sound to Gieben Mine.

Dwarfs were spread out, under trees, coughing and panting, and wiping their faces with handkerchiefs. Dust from the cave mouth hung heavy; some of it wafted skyward. Baugi laid beside a bush. His right leg was splinted.

"Baugi! What happened?" Anya and Max knelt down.

"A cave in! I only hope all the men got out in time!" He coughed.

"What happened to your leg, Baugi?" Max asked.

"Broke it. Minecart fell on me two days ago."

Baugi said bad things had been going on at the mine. The owner started making everyone's labor harder, and he added two hours to the workday. Accidents started happening because the miners were worn out, and felt rushed. Which is how Baugi's leg broke: the foreman made the men push the minecarts too fast and one of them derailed, falling on Baugi.

"But why'd the mine cave in?"

"Drilling too deep without putting up more braces. Thank goodness before the main ceiling gave out, the ground trembled long enough for most of us to get out!"

"We felt the ground rumbling, near Drammend," Max said.

Shouting came from the cave. "Help! Someone, help me, please?"

Max and Anya jumped up. Max grabbed the pick axe and Anya the shovel. They unhooked the wagon from Hilde. "Hilde, come!"

"Anya! Max, no! Don't go in there! It might collapse again! No—come back!" Baugi tried to get up, but his splinted leg made it impossible to stop them.

They followed the voice to a distance half a stone's throw from the entrance. In rubble, and half buried were two boots and part of a leg. One arm stuck out and above it, an opening large enough to see a face. Anya went to it. There, two desperate eyes peeked out from a face covered in dust.

"Can you get me outta here?" the victim said. Max and Anya started rolling off the rocks. They didn't use their tools, lest they injure him. With the rocks removed, however, they saw part of a beam angled on his stomach. He was pinned.

They needed help but didn't have time to call for it—the cave might collapse again. They yanked, and pushed and heaved the beam, but it barely moved. Lucky for them, a worker from outside ran in. With the strength of three people straining and pushing, the beam slid off. The injured man grunted and hoisted himself forward. He looked dazed.

The worker and Max tried to pull him to his feet.

"Come on, Geirod, help us, big guy!" his co-worker said. "Over here!" Max pointed to Hilde's back.

Geirod cried out, and slumped his large body over Hilde's back. His feet dangled on one side, almost touching the ground. His head bobbled on the other side.

Anya knew donkeys to be strong enough to carry almost two times their weight. But this was a very large load. The worker pulled Hilde's rope and Max and Anya each supported one of the man's feet, to lighten Hilde's load. Step over step, Hilde plodded to Baugi. They slid the man to the ground and laid him down. He went unconscious.

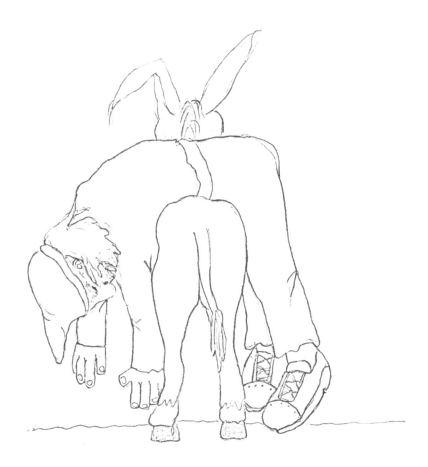

A second rumbling began, deep within the cavern. Then came the sounds of rocks grinding on each other. Everyone stared. Smoke and dust billowed from its mouth.

Baugi looked at Max and Anya. "Children, you saved Geirod just in time! And Slav, thank you!" Baugi shook hands with his co-worker. He reached for Hilde's muzzle. "You, too, Hilde!"

Baugi gazed at the victim. "Children, this is my neighbor. Geirod's a giant dwarf."

The children didn't even know giant dwarfs existed. Was Baugi teasing? They studied Geirod. He definitely was no ordinary dwarf, being twice as tall as Baugi. His shoulders were broad, his upper arms muscular and he barely had a neck. His feet were long and wide, but his fingers were short and stubby, like Baugi's. They'd never seen anyone like him.

Embla and Njord arrived, driving a large wagon. As soon as Embla stopped, she climbed down and ran to her husband to make sure he was alright. Several of the miners carried Baugi and Geirod aboard the wagon, using planks. Embla offered many of the dwarfs a ride.

Baugi called Anya and Max to his side. "Children, thank you for helping today." He squeezed something into their hands and closed their fingers around it. "Put it in your pockets and look at it after supper, will you?'

They thanked him.

Embla kissed their faces and tussled Hilde's head. When she drove off with the wagonload of workers, everyone waved good-bye.

On the way home, Hilde noticed a small cave off the main road. It was pint size compared to the Gieben mine. They ate their lunch and started digging. They went as far in as they dared and dug a deep hole. They unearthed a hammer, a harness bell and an old coin. The coin had scrollwork and a hole in the middle. They thought their finds were worthless.

Anya remembered what Grandmum said, though: "Hope springs eternal." There's always a next time as long as you have legs to walk and eyes to see.

CHAPTER FIVE

A Royal Visit

The Tamarkins tried to keep the news about Hilde quiet. Mother's little chat over a cup of tea with her neighbor, however, didn't stop Mrs. Petrov. She wasn't a quiet lady. And Grandmum confessed that she told her neighbor. Before long, all sorts of people knew. No one was surprised anymore when Hilde spoke.

King Gregory heard about it and summoned them to the castle. Majadonia was a good day's ride from Bergen, and the Tamarkins had no carriage. The king graciously sent one of his and a carrier for Hilde. Freddy and Katia stayed with Grandmum, while they were gone.

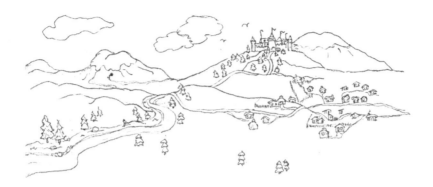

At the castle, a servant ushered them into the throne room. Anya scanned it from ceiling to floor and side to side. The floor was like glass. It shone softly, not with a glare that hurts the eyes. A chandelier hung over the thrones, dangling with green jewels. Anya did a double take. Were they peridots? There were beautiful paintings adorning both walls and a portrait on the back wall of an older king and queen. The thrones themselves stood upon a dais placed to the left of the portrait. Each armed chair was upholstered in velvet, his was royal purple, hers the color of red wine.

"Welcome, Mr. Tamarkin and family. Come in," said King Gregory.

"How do you do, your Majesty," said Garth, Günter and Anya in unison (as their parents instructed). They bowed and curtsied.

"Allow me to introduce my wife. This is Queen Sasha the Watchful." She rose from her chair and her cream dress with layers of silk made a luscious rustling sound. They were invited to come nearer.

Queen Sasha's golden hair was fashionably pinned upon her head and encircled by her tiara. Her cheeks were blush, and she wore a single strand choker of sparkling gems. Anya and her brothers were spellbound. Garth reached to kiss her hand and Papa pulled him back.

Anya whispered to her mother, "Look what we're standing on, Mama." She thought the rug beneath their feet was the most beautiful thing ever. It was rectangle shaped, bordered in cream, and fringed. Its middle held another rectangle, in which continuous cream swirls interwove with orange-red and wine-red poppies. It was warm and stately, at the same time. She alternated looking at the rug and staring at the queen, back and forth.

"Mr. and Mrs. Tamarkin. Might I meet your children?"

Brief introductions followed. Garth and Günter never took their eyes off Queen Sasha.

King Gregory clapped and a servant ushered Hilde in on a gold rope. Bathed and brushed, she looked wonderful. Her tail was wound with a ribbon.

The king said, "I've heard that this remarkable donkey can talk. Is this true?"

The family turned to Hilde, and let her respond.

"*Yes, sir king. It true. I speak some words,*" Hilde said. She nickered softly.

His eyes went large.

Queen Sasha said, "Oh my! Then it's true! And isn't this glorious?" She clasped her hands.

King Gregory said he thought Hilde could do a lot of good for Bergen and Gieben if she were to enlist in his army as an "informant." She could watch and report anything out of the ordinary to Vera. For this and the care Father and Mother might promise to give her, they would be paid.

"You needn't do that, Your Majesty. We love Hilde and do all that, already."

"Unless I do, I don't feel right. This way, she earns her keep and pledges herself to my service."

He turned to Hilde. "Hilde, do you want to be an informant in my service?"

Hilde brayed and said, "*Yes, king sir.*"

King Gregory smiled, removed his sword and said, "Then, Hilde The Talking Donkey, I dub thee High Soldier of King Gregory, Defender of Men, to protect the middle villages, serving as my informant." He touched Hilde's right shoulder with the tip of the sword, then her left.

Hilde trembled, wiggled her tail and chittered.

This ceremonial act, and Hilde's response moved Anya to tears.

"Oh, sweet girl! Don't cry! Your donkey shall not leave your side. She's still yours!" said Queen Sasha.

Anya shook her head. "No, my queen, it isn't that. It's how happy you've made Hilde."

The king and queen smiled. He spoke to Father. "Sir, will you sign a contract to let Hilde serve me?"

Father swallowed hard and nodded. Günter wiped an eye.

The king unfurled the document:

Let it hereby be known in all of Majadon Kingdom

That from henceforth and evermore

Hilde the Talking Donkey, belonging to Anya Tamarkin & her family shall be the High Soldier of King Gregory the Watchful, Majadon

Thereby earning her owner a stipend,
to be paid monthly

Signed: King Gregory, Defender of Men &
Queen Sasha, The Watchful

Agreed: _____
Gaillard Tamarkin, father

Agreed: _____
Anya Tamarkin, owner

Father took the quill, dipped into the inkwell and signed, with a trembling hand.

"And now, Anya? If you have no objections, I need your signature under your father's, please?"

Anya was smitten. Her bottom lip quivered. The king was honoring her, too?

Father whispered, "It's all right, Anya. Sign here." He pointed to her line and she wrote the best signature she could. Her hand shook.

The next day, the king and queen gave them a tour of Majadonia. They rode in the royal carriage through the streets. Watching the people from the inside of the carriage, as the king and queen drove by with their four prancing white horses and coachman felt like something out of a dream. People cheered and waved and Hilde trotted along behind them with the coachman's son on her back. Anya knew Hilde was proud to be in King Gregory's service.

They rode to the river, and through the countryside to see the many farms and grazing lands. Even the sheep bleated loudly at the procession. The king pointed out a mine on the mountain where gold excavating was in progress. The thatched cottages up and down the roads looked cozy, and there were run-down huts, too. All the people seemed happy to live there.

After a peaceful night's sleep in rooms too wonderful to describe, it was time to depart. The queen sent along some food. They set out for Bergen, for Mama wanted to be home by nightfall.

Anya knew she'd never forget this day as long as she lived.

CHAPTER SIX

The Wonderful Treasure

Hilde was happy and asked to go to Bergen and Gieben and tell the villagers the big news. Anya couldn't blame her. She did need to explain her role. She and Max went along, for they would dig for more treasure, afterwards. Maybe today they'd find peridot, or something else wonderful.

Everyone was delighted to see Hilde, for no other donkey in the land was like her. She handled almost anything, or at least tried. Like carrying the giant out of the mine. In fact, she often carried heavy loads for people along the highway. She pulled wagons in orchards, gave rides to children, helped poor farmers plow, and carried food baskets from the market balanced on her sides. And Hilde's sense of humor was delightful. She came up with a dance routine she performed for willing audiences. She would shuffle left, then right, and cross and uncross her feet. It didn't matter if she stumbled or fell; either way, she brought gales of laughter.

When they finished Hilde's announcement tour, they walked north. They entered The Enchanted Forest, and sat in its shade beside a creek. They'd brought the wagon and tools, and another picnic lunch even if they didn't have krumkakes. When they finished eating, they washed their hands and feet in the cool waters.

Hilde chased some ducks until they flew back to the creek, then laid on her back and rolled in the grass. She knew how to have a good time.

Anya and Max took out their tools and went to work. Within minutes, they heard a clunk. Max laid down his shovel.

Anya took out a claw tool and slowly dragged clumps of dirt away. Was it an old dish? She lifted it out; no, a ceramic pitcher. Still in one piece, it had a crack near its spout. Anya fondled it. "Max! This is valuable."

"Nah, it's only a dumb pouring jug."

"Well, Grandmum will know." She laid it inside her leather hat, in the wagon.

"I wish I'd find something interesting." He picked his shovel back up.

Hilde was sniffing the creek bank and making noises.

They ran over. There in the bank was a large hole. Hilde's hooves were covered with dirt.

"Did you find something, Hilde?"

She brayed.

Max dug deeper and Anya helped until they saw the emergence of something white. Max worked around it. Before long, it looked to be the top of a bone. A gigantic bone they couldn't get under. Max put his hand on hers, to stop her from digging. "We need grown-ups to get this out, Anya. This is really big. It could be an animal that lived a long time ago."

"Or it could be an elephant whose cargo ship got lost at sea and landed here!" She didn't believe Max.

Max didn't laugh. "No, Anya, this isn't funny. My grandfather said there used to be giant lizards here. And mastodons."

"Oh." Anya stopped teasing. "Well! If these bones are hundreds of years old, we better do something to protect them, shouldn't we?"

"We most definitely should." Max grabbed his shovel and starting pitching dirt back in the hole. "Come on, help! We've got to hide this."

"But who can we trust with this, Max?"

"My papa or yours can find someone to—wait! They can go straight to the king. That's the smartest plan."

Anya nodded, "Yes, our king always does the right thing. They can send Vera to deliver the news." She picked up her shovel.

They filled the hole, and scattered rocks and branches over it, to make it look like debris.

*   *   *

After supper, Anya pulled out Baugi's gift. A blue-green gemstone! She ran to show Papa—could it be peridot? She could hardly wait to thank Baugi and find out. Perhaps he could make a necklace with it. Papa gave her a small wooden box. In it, she tucked away small things for safekeeping and slid the box beneath the bed. Perhaps one day she'd get a pretty treasure box—with painted fairies on the outside, and cushioned silk on the inside.

Max and Anya showed Günter their finds. He thought the only things of value were the coin and the pitcher. Anya told Max to keep the whorl, and gave the pitcher to her grandmother.

The news of their discovery was reported straight away to King Gregory. In a fortnight, his workers started an official excavation, and from the earth came the skeleton of a giant lizard that stood on its hind two feet. It was thought to be thousands of years old. When Anya and Max saw an illustration, they were astounded.

"Look what we found!" Max exclaimed.

"You mean, look what Hilde found," Anya corrected him.

*   *   *

The next week, Grandmum asked Anya and Max to come by. She wanted to hear about their treasure hunting. Anya noticed the brown pitcher on her shelf.

Grandmum listened carefully. "Sounds like your search was successful, chilblains."

"Not really, Nonni. We still haven't found gold or peridot. And I don't think we ever will." Anya looked down.

Max reached into his pocket. "Anya, you can't say that. We've barely started. And I like what we found so far." He pulled out the whorl and laid it on his palm. "This is a treasure. And thanks to Hilde, so is the giant lizard! Majadon's loaded with more treasure. I just know it!"

"Well, maybe you're right, Max."

"Oh, my yes, Anya." Grandmum pointed to the shelf. "Look at that pitcher. It's just one of a hundred more treasures. My great-grandmother had one like this, from her grandparents. And you gave it to me." Her eyes welled with tears.

"Nonni! Don't cry." Anya put her arms around her.

69

"Oh, I'm all right." Her grandmother patted her arm. "But don't stop looking, honey. You must persist. You never know what you'll find next."

A glint came to Anya's eyes. "I have a treasure box, Nonni; Papa made me a wooden one. I have two things in it, so far."

"Well, how about that." Grandmum clasped her hands.

Max's eyebrows arched. "Well, what are they?"

"All right. I'll tell you." She paused. "First is Baugi's gemstone. May I ask what he gave you, Max?"

"A gold piece."

"I think he gave us these from his heart, Max."

"I know," Max rolled his eyes.

"The second treasure is the red silk cord and note that came with Hilde."

"Aw, honey." Grandmum held out her arms and Anya nestled within them.

A honk came from Grandmum's parlor. They went around the corner to see what it was. The curtains flapped in the open window, framing Hilde. Her chin laid on its high ledge. *"Anya, you my treasure!"*

Anya ran to her and cradled her face. "And Hilde, you're mine!"

*   *   *

Hilde faithfully patrols Bergen and parts of Enchanted Forest. Anya is certain if there's danger, she will detect it. She understands Hilde now, and doesn't mind sharing her with Majadon. Hilde walks behind the cottages or in and out of the forest. She enjoys walking the riverbanks and climbing the hills for better views. Her daily plodding has formed trails everywhere. Villagers use them for hikes and shortcuts, and everyone calls them Hilde's Trails.

Hilde seems to favor Grandmum's cottage, for she visits there several times a week. Before long, Anya learned why. Hilde found a friend in Finn, Grandmum's jack. The two of them are pals.

They frolic and romp in the fields, roll in the grass and smell the flowers. If they are near the fence, their chittering at each other amuses passersby.

Their favorite spot is beneath Grandmum's largest oak, and they sometimes rest there for hours. Hilde's come of age, and Grandmum thinks there shall be a new little Hilde or Finn next year, in the magical kingdom of Majadon.

Anya's so excited, she wonders how she'll endure waiting for such another wonderful treasure.

GLOSSARY and CHARACTERS

aggressive (ə-grĕs´ iv), *adj.* Bold or harsh behavior.

aghast (ə-găst´), *adj.* Shock or amazement.

bray (brā) *n. or v.* The sound of a donkey or to utter the sound a donkey makes.

bridle (brid´), *n.* A harness with a headstall, bit and reins fitted about a horse or donkey's head to restrain or guide it.

budge (bŭj) , *v.* To move slightly.

ceremonial (sĕr-ə-mō′nē-əl), *adj.* Use of a format act or ritual.

chilblain (chil ´ blān), *n.* Nickname for a dearly loved Norwegian child.

chitter (chĭt´ ər), *v.* To twitter like a bird, high-pitched.

chutter/ing (chŭt´ tər), *v.* Fluttery throat noises donkeys make.

commotion (kə-mō′ shən), n. A disturbance, a civil disorder.

compliant/complied (kŏm-plīd′)/comply, *adj.* or *v.* To go along with another's wish.

cooperate (kŏ-ŏp′-ə-rāt), *v.* To work together willingly for a common good.

crinkled (krĭn′gkəd), *v.* Creases made in the skin of a face

dais (dā′ əs), *n.* A raised platform, not high.

disheveled (dĭ-shĕv-ld), *adj.* Untidy.

embers (ĕm′bər), *n.* Burning or glowing coal or wood in a dying fire.

emissary (ĕm′ ĭ-sər′-ē), *n.* Someone sent on a mission to represent the interest of another.

excavation (ex′-ka-vā-shŭn), *n.* A removal of something hidden, usually dug from the earth.

feudal (fyoo′ dl), *adj.* Receiving a piece of land in return for farming it, after a certain time.

fortnight (fôrt′ nīt), *n.* 14 days.

frolick/ed (fro-lĭk), *v.* Fun, merriment, a carefree time.

furrowed (für′ ōd), *v.* Forehead marked with lines or crinkles.

harness (här´nĭs), *n.* The gear used on a work animal to pull or direct something.

hitch/ed (hĭch), *v.* or *n.* To connect or fasten two things together.

jack (jăk), *n.* A male donkey.

jenny (jĕn´ nē), *n.* A female donkey.

Krumkake (krŭm kä´ kə), *n.* A Norwegian curved waffle cookie that can be stuffed.

Latkes (lät´ kə), *n.* A pancake usually made of grated potatoes.

lull/ed (lŭl), *v.* To cause to sleep, soothe or calm.

menacingly (mĕn´ ĭs-ĭng-lē), *adv.* To cause threat or trouble to someone.

nicker/ed (nik´ ər), *v.* A horse or donkey sound showing happiness.

nuzzle (nŭz´ əl), *v.* To rub or push against gently with the nose or snout; to nestle together.

obedient (ŏ-bē´-dē-ĕnt), *adj.* To do as you are told, to follow the rules.

paddy wagon, *n.* A wagon or van used to transport prisoners or captured creatures.

parroted (pär ́ət-ĕd), *v.* To imitate or repeat words of another, usually without understanding.

persist/ed (pər-sĭst), *v.* To keep at something, not give up.

pike (pēk ́-yā), *n.* A nickname for beloved one.

remarkable (rē-mär′kē-bəl), *adj.* Striking.

respectable (rĕs-pĕk ́ tä-bül), *adj.* To show honor, have integrity, to follow the law.

ruble (rū ́ bül), *n.* A Russian coin worth about one penny.

ruckus (rŭ′ kəs), *n.* A disturbance or commotion.

stipend (stī′ pĕnd), *n.* A sum paid as a salary.

strain/ed (strānd), *v. or adj.* Stretched or forced beyond limits.

summon (sŭm′mən), *v.* Urgently call someone to be present.

swivel/ed (swĭ ́ vəl), *v.* To pivot, turn or rotate.

tunic (tōō ́ nĭk), *n.* A loose-fitting garment worn to the knees.

whorl (whôrl), *n.* A metal coin with a center hole, decorated. Value unknown.

ABOUT THE AUTHOR

Deborah Thomas has written songs and poems for children and adult devotionals for years. Writing and illustrating the Anya tales has fulfilled a lifelong dream. *Anya's Remarkable Donkey* is the second fairy story in the Anya series, inspired by a memorable donkey named Jack, a temporary childhood pet in Michigan.

Born in Grand Rapids, she loved small town community life and spent summers on Big Lake, surrounded by farms. Today, she has a bungalow in nearby Allegan, and enjoys getaway time reminiscent of her former lifestyle.

Feeling fortunate to attend Biola College and the University of Arizona, she graduated in 1970. After retiring, she chose substitute teaching to stay connected to children, and teaches piano from home. She remarried in 2000, and her twelfth grandchild was born this year. Besides these delights, she and her husband are raising two rescue dogs, Pippa and Lucy-Hazel.

At every moment possible you'll find Deborah writing her next story. You can reach her at tdthomas2000@gmail.com and read her blog at deborahjthomas.com.

ACKNOWLEDGMENTS

The unfolding and final edition of this story is owed, with deep appreciation, to the following persons.

Interior layout, KDP technician and back cover: Benjamin Vrbicek

Graphic artist and book cover: Monty Kugler

Illustrations: art books and artisans that inspired the author

Moral support: Karen Kirkland, faithful sister, Victoria Bergesen, patient friend and Elisa Gruss and children: Rowen, Asher, Eleora and Enoch, enthusiastic cheerleaders.

Professional and editing readers: Callista and Victoria Bergesen, Penny Cheshier, Marcia Cook, Abrielle De Vault, Karen Kirkland, Julie Maniglia, and Lisa Periale Martin

Endorsements: Abrielle DeVault and Penny Cheshier

Encouragement: Positive support from my
husband Terry Thomas, and two wonderful
groups: my book club lit lovers and Grace
Community friends.

Made in the USA
Middletown, DE
18 February 2022